Dear Parent:
Your child's love of reading starts here!

Every child learns to read in a different way and at his or her own speed. Some go back and forth between reading levels and read favorite books again and again. Others read through each level in order. You can help your young reader improve and become more confident by encouraging his or her own interests and abilities. From books your child reads with you to the first books he or she reads alone, there are I Can Read Books for every stage of reading:

SHARED READING
Basic language, word repetition, and whimsical illustrations, ideal for sharing with your emergent reader

BEGINNING READING
Short sentences, familiar words, and simple concepts for children eager to read on their own

READING WITH HELP
Engaging stories, longer sentences, and language play for developing readers

READING ALONE
Complex plots, challenging vocabulary, and high-interest topics for the independent reader

ADVANCED READING
Short paragraphs, chapters, and exciting themes for the perfect bridge to chapter books

I Can Read Books have introduced children to the joy of reading since 1957. Featuring award-winning authors and illustrators and a fabulous cast of beloved characters, I Can Read Books set the standard for beginning readers.

A lifetime of discovery begins with the magical words **"I Can Read!"**

Visit www.icanread.com for information
on enriching your child's reading experience.

Special book thanks
to Tamar Mays, and
Minnesota snowy-day
thanks to A.D. and B.W.
—S.M.

For John Schindel,
fellow traveler
—J.K.M.W.

I Can Read Book® is a trademark of HarperCollins Publishers.

Library of Congress Cataloging-in-Publication Data is available.
ISBN 978-0-06-147370-8 (trade bdg.)   ISBN 978-0-06-147372-2 (pbk.)

11 12 13 14 15   SCP   10 9 8 7 6 5 4 3 2 1   ❖   First Edition

I Can Read!

READING
2
WITH HELP

Zack's Alligator

and the First Snow

WITHDRAWN

story by Shirley Mozelle
pictures by James Watts

HARPER

An Imprint of HarperCollinsPublishers

The lake was frozen solid.

Dad and Mom were ice fishing.

Zack stayed on the bank.

He began to build a snowman.

Snow got into Zack's pockets.

He felt Bridget move.

Bridget was an alligator key chain

that grew when she got wet.

Uncle Jim had sent her from Florida.

Bridget crawled out of Zack's pocket.

"Hi, Zack!" she said.

Bridget grew bigger and bigger.

Soon Bridget was fully grown.

Bridget looked around.

She saw something

she had never seen before.

"Zack! The sky is falling,"

she said.

"That's snow," said Zack.

"There are lots of flakes of snow.

Each one is different."

"Oh," said Bridget. "Like the snails

and slugs in the Glades."

Zack and Bridget danced and twirled.

A girl came running over.

"Cool! A magic snow alligator!"

she said.

Bridget shivered.

"I'm not cool.

I'm cold," Bridget said.

So the girl gave Bridget her scarf.

"Let's make snow angels," said Zack.

Bridget lay on her back like Zack.

Zack made snow angels.

Bridget made gator angels.

The girl made angels too.

Zack, Bridget, and the girl

opened their mouths to catch snow.

"Zack!" said Bridget.

"Snow is cold and melty.

But I am hungry, not thirsty."

Bridget stopped and sniffed the air.

"I smell something fishy,"

she said to Zack.

Bridget ran onto the lake.

Bump! Down she went.

"Zack!" said Bridget.

"This snow is as slippery as slime."

"You are on ice," said Zack.

Bridget got her balance.

She wobbled.

She followed the fishy smell.

Dad poured Mom a cup of coffee.

Suddenly there was a huge splash.

"Wow!" said Dad.

"That must have been a big fish!"

Mom and Dad went to get dry clothes.

18

Bridget swam in the cold water.

She caught all the fish she wanted.

She wanted all the fish she saw.

Bridget got out of the water.

She burped a gator burp.

"Gator pardons!" she said.

Bridget danced and sang.

"Fish! Fish! Fish!

I love lots of wet, cold fish!"

Then Bridget spotted something.

"That's a snowman," Zack told her.

"Hello, snowman!" said Bridget.

The snowman did not answer.

"Zack," said Bridget,

"this snowman is frozen."

Bridget put the scarf

around the snowman's neck.

"Let's go sledding!" said Zack.

Bridget hopped onto a sled.

She zoomed past the trees.

Then Bridget ran off the path.

She landed in the snow.

"I was flying, Zack!" she said.

Zack saw that Bridget

was starting to shrink.

Zack and Bridget sat on the sled.

It began to get dark.

"The snow is twinkly," said Bridget.

"Like the stars."

Bridget leaned closer to Zack.

She shrank smaller and smaller.

"We had fun," said Bridget.

"We sure did," said Zack.

Zack heard his father.

"No fish today," said his dad.

"Not a one."

"How was sledding?" asked Mom.

"Great!" said Zack. "Bridget and I . . ."

"Bridget?" asked Dad.

"The alligator key chain, dear,"
Mom said.

Dad saw the key chain on Zack's lap.

"I guess Bridget ate

all the fish today!" said Dad.

"Probably," said Zack.

Zack put Bridget in his pocket.
"We'll have more fun soon,"
he whispered.